Dreaming of Noelle

ENCHANTED WISHES COLLECTION

VIOLA TEMPEST

VIOLA TEMPEST PUBLISHING

Copyright

Dreaming of Noelle

Enchanted Wishes Collection

© Copyright 2023 Viola Tempest

Cover Design by Fay Lane Cover Design

Contents

Dreaming of NOELLE

of

ENCHANTED WISHES COLLECTION

VIOLA TEMPEST

If only I'd known. If only I hadn't been so naïve. So stupid and naïve! Thinking someone like me could ever be with someone like her... well, not again, anyway. I did have it all, once, but then it disappeared as soon as it came into my life. Such a fool. Such a fool.

The days get colder and colder here in this cabin, the nights almost unbearable. Why'd I think living a life in the North Pole of Fairbanks, Alaska was ever a good idea? Such an idiot! I've never been a fan of the cold.

Ever since I graduated from a prestigious university in the north, I'd gone as south as south could get. Texas was a good choice for a while, but even that soon got to be too chilly, and I hauled my ass over to Arizona, where my parents live. Smart. Hell, if Death Valley allowed occupants, I might've just moved there, too. And Erica always came along for the ride, hating the cold just as much as I did.

But that's all just a passing thought now, a memory that will forever stay just a memory. With no transportation, a fallen dream, and a girlfriend I'll never see again, I've lost hope in ever trying to get out of here. Sigh, this is my home now, this cold wooden abyss that's barely able to hold itself up against the angry, raging winds, let alone an entire human being residing in it.

But honestly, if I could go back in time and take it all back, make sure I don't go down the path that I did, I'm not so sure I would. She was everything, my Christmas miracle, and I'd give anything to have her back in my arms.

I turn around and look behind me, sighing again. Guess I'll need more firewood soon, but what's the point anymore?

It's rough enough venturing out there in the dead of winter, risking frostbite to gather frozen wood in my arms. But even so, I'll only just be prolonging my own death. This suffering gets unbearable most of the time, and I don't know how much more I can take. Many nights, I try to close my eyes, try to bring back the image of the girl who once was, but for some reason, she doesn't return. She doesn't seem to ever return.

The rose on my desk, the very same rose I'd given to her the day we became official, I'll never forget. It's the only thing I have left that reminds me of her, and no way in hell am I going to let that just crumple also, much like my heart. She promised me a lifetime of happiness, living together forever, my wish finally coming true.

And of course, I had to be so naïve. I had to trust every pair of walking heel who came in my direction and flashed me a smile. The same thing happened with Erica, and the same thing is happening now.

So, why do I keep trying to convince myself that Noelle's different? That she's not like Erica. That's she's sweet and genuine, that she truly loves me for me.

Why do I keep holding onto the hope that she'll come back, that she really is my Christmas miracle? Why can't I just let go?

I used to love the holidays, especially Christmas. The chimes of carolers singing. The bells of mistletoes ringing. The harmonious laughter of joyful children as they danced around the brightly decorated tree in front of City Hall. And it didn't matter to me one bit that there was never any snow. I did live in a desert, after all, the lukewarm temperature giving off a summer vibe rather than a winter one. But nope, didn't matter to me one bit.

I had everything I needed, with or without the snow and frigid winter. My career was finally kicking off. My brother just had a baby, and Erica and I were due to have one soon, too. My mother almost had a heart attack when we told her Erica was carrying.

"Before you're married?!" she gasped and pretended to fall over in her usual overdramatic fashion.

But Dad was always there to catch her, right before her head hit anything beside the throw pillows. Sometimes I wonder whether they'd still be together if he'd let her fall once, just once. Probably not. Mom's overdramatic, but she's also the most ruthless person I'd ever met in my entire life, and I'm not just saying that because she's my mother.

The year was 2018, that was going to be my best Christmas ever. Wanna know why? It was the year I finally asked Erica to be, not only the mother of my child, but also my wife. She'd been hinting at it for a while. I could read her like a book. She'd been texting her girlfriends for the past several months, going out late with them and coming home at wee hours in the morning. I knew it was because she'd wanted to get their opinions on how long it'd take me before I finally popped the question. They were all married, after all. It just made sense.

I knew. Like I said, I could read her like a book... or so I thought.

That look she gave me when I got down on one knee and popped the question was one I will never be able to get out of my head. A look of pure disgust, like she was completely fine with having my baby but wanted to hurl at the thought of having to look at my face every day. Women, can't live with them, and they certainly didn't want to live with me.

Turns out, all those hints I'd been getting weren't hints to propose. They were hints to break up. All those nights she'd spent texting her girlfriends and going out with them for advice, she'd been seeing some guy named Milton behind my back. A co-worker, she'd tried to pass off as at first, but it didn't take long before I found out that she'd met him at my brother's baby shower. What the hell kind of name is Milton, anyway? The curses just never stop coming, do they? Just my luck.

And there she went. Packed up the little suitcase that she had and walked right out the door... the morning of Christmas day. Christmas hadn't been the same since. Two more had gone by, and that Christmas spirit I'd been so fond of, right out the door and straight into a fire pit. By the time the third one rolled around, my friends and family had grown sick of me.

"Just get over her already," they'd say to me. "It's been three fucking years. Just get over her and move on."

If you haven't guessed it, that only added fuel to my anger. For six years, we'd been together, Freshman year in college and dating ever since. Not to mention that she had my own flesh and blood sitting inside that filthy womb of hers... at least, I hope that was my child. What did it matter anymore? She was gone... off to batshit nowhere, and that restraining order she'd gotten against me certainly didn't help in me trying to find her.

But I still tried. I still loved her. Of course, I did. For nearly three years, I continued trying to bring her back into my life, looking her up on the Internet and bugging the hell out of friends. I'd be lucky if I found someone to help me. Most of them just shut me out, saying I was bringing them down and ruining their holiday spirit. The hypocrisy. Others, the rare few, only agreed to help me if I got the hell out of their homes. But even still, I never found her. She's out there some-where with my child, and there's no way I can get in touch with her.

"Will you snap out of it?" My brother, Mark,

yelled over in my direction and tossed a few popcorn kernels at me.

The year was now 2021, and those few weeks before Christmas changed my life forever.

I picked up the kernels, ate a couple, and tossed the rest back over at him. "Dude, stop! You're wasting food!" I exclaimed.

But he just shrugged. "Eh, the dog will take care of it. He's a garbage disposal. It's why we named him that."

"It's why *you* named him that. Mom and Dad named him Rufus, remember?"

"Yeah." Mark shrugged. "But that name's dumb. I like Garbage much, much better."

I rolled my eyes at him and reached over to the tree to pluck off a candy cane. I figured the more I ate, the less there'd be left when the actual day rolled around. Plus, it didn't hurt that I also have a sweet tooth when it comes to peppermint.

"Of course, you would. He's the animal equivalent of you. I'm surprised Shanna doesn't hide the food so you wouldn't eat it all."

"Mom! Max's being an asshole again!" he called out to our mother, who was making chili in the kitchen.

"Settle down, boys," she said on autopilot. Then she

stepped out into the living room, the garlic-coated ladle still in her hand, sauce slowly dripping onto the hardwood floor. "You two are grown men. I didn't invite you over here for lunch just so you can throw popcorn at each other. Now, clean up the mess. Chili's ready."

Mark watched as Mom walked back into the kitchen, then turned around and stuck his tongue out at me, as if he'd just won. I grumbled back at him and walked into the kitchen to help Mom, snagging a taste of the first scoop before he had a chance to. That was usually my way of getting revenge.

Things didn't get much easier as the days went by. The closer and closer we got to Christmas, the more bitter I became. All around me, including the office, restaurants, and parks, everyone was starting to get into that holiday spirit, with their tinsel and billions of ornaments. I wanted to vomit. The cheerfulness and colorful lights gave me an even bigger migraine than the one I had the day Erica walked out. It was all just so... so... sickening.

When I walked into the office twelve days before, everyone was already dressed in ugly green and red sweaters, getting drunk on the eggnog in their hands, and handing out Santa hats for everyone else to get into that festive mood. I grabbed one, sat down at my desk, and threw it in the trash. I didn't want any part in the celebration. The eggnog, I did drink, however;

the chilled liquid running down my throat was enough to ease my anxiety for a time being. Anything I could do to make this awful month pass by that much faster was a good thing, in my opinion.

"Ho! Ho! Ho!" my boss, Peter Sands, said as he came over to my desk.

I could smell the stench of eggnog on his breath, the egg whites coating the mustache on his upper lip, and the cinnamon powder blowing from his mouth whenever he coughed. Disgusting. I tried to turn my body away so none of it would get on me, but turned out that it didn't matter. Most of it didn't reach past the belly of his white dress shirt and paisley tie. Those, paired with his thick framed glasses, showed the man's true lack of style. But then again, it didn't' seem like he had anyone in his life to tell him otherwise.

"Mr. Miller," he continued. "You know, being antisocial isn't going to get you bonus points with the boss, especially not when your boss is the life of the party."

"Sorry, sir. I'm not being antisocial. I just have a lot of work to get done."

But Peter wouldn't have it. He pushed back my chair and sat his lard of an ass down on my desk, smacked on top of the notebook I was writing in.

"Nope!" he chimed. "Today, your job is to join the party and have fun!" Then his jolly smile turned into a cold, death glare. "Do it, or you're fired," followed by another jolly laugh. "I'm just messing with you. Come! Join the others. Grab a slice of cake. Enjoy yourself!"

It all seemed so innocent, but I knew what he was trying to do. Steer me away from my work so he could berate me later for not getting everything done. It's one of the cruelest tricks in the book.

"No, thanks," I shook my head and said again. "I have a lot of work to do."

He let out a vociferous laugh, then patted me on the back. "Ha! Suit yourself, party pooper."

Four agonizing hours later, I was finally able to get into my car and drive home. It would've taken an army to squeeze past the drunk crowd blocking the entire front entrance. But it didn't bother me... especially not when I was so desperate that the fire exit seemed like the much better option. They'd deal with the alarm after I was long gone. Didn't need me.

When I finally got home, I threw my briefcase on top of my couch, the remote that was resting there bouncing off and onto the floor.

"Whatever," I muttered, then proceeded into the kitchen to have my own party, a pack of cigarettes and a bottle of whiskey.

It's all I needed lately. Mark tried to set me up every now and then, the next gold digger always worse than the last, and it got to the point where I'd just roll my eyes, get their number, and never reach out. They're all the same, just another heartbreaker, much like Erica.

The nights alone had been getting harder and harder lately. I'd debated getting a puppy, something to keep me company, but with my luck, it'd just leave me, too. My shitty unlovable life.

When the butt of the cigarette went out, I downed the rest of my whiskey. When that was finished... what then?

Angrily, I smashed the glass bottle against my balcony, glass shards spilling across the ground, and then held the jagged edges to my wrist. I could do it. One swift motion, and the hell I was living in would all be over. No one would ever need to know. Not like anyone ever visited. And even if they did find out, who cares? I'd be dead anyway.

The glass moved closer toward my bare arm, veins popping and forehead sweating.

"Just one swift motion," I kept telling myself, but the more I tried to push, the more my body resisted.

Finally, the anxiety became too overwhelming, and I threw the remaining half of the bottle off my balcony, hearing it shatter on the street of downtown Phoenix before retreating into my room and climbing into bed.

"Maybe tomorrow will be better."

It usually never was.

Chapter Two

"Max, Max, wake up."

My eyes sprung open to the sound of a female voice. "Huh? Who's there?"

But at first glance, I found that I was no longer in my own room, nor in my own apartment. The plain white walls that I had been so used to had suddenly transformed into ones of crimson red that surrounded a room of holiday decorations. At first, I thought I'd been kidnapped. That my dad or brother had come into my apartment in the middle of the night and dragged me out to celebrate Christmas with them.

But when the female voice walked out, I'd nearly shit my pants.

"Erica?" I asked. "Why are you here? I never thought I'd see you again."

My brain felt as though it was spinning in circles. I'd spent years chasing down my ex, with no luck, and suddenly, she was standing in a vomit-inducing room wearing a Santa hat and carrying a platter full of chocolate chip cookies.

The woman smiled at me. The way her freshly-painted lips curved upwards reminded me of why I'd fallen in love with Erica in the first place. But then she spoke, and my brain spun even more.

"No, Max. I'm Noelle, and I'm glad I finally found you," the woman said.

I'd nearly shit my pants again at the disbelief. It couldn't be. Erica never mentioned a sister, much less a twin. I shook my head. No, I would've known if she had one. I knew everything about her... well, almost everything. Milton. Fuck him.

"Who... who are you?" I managed to stutter. "Where... where am I?"

I carefully backed away as she inched closer. The plastic ornaments and fake snow strewn over the living room floor definitely made it harder than it needed to be. And even as I stumbled into a corner, she continued closing in, finally reaching down and placing a hand on my knee.

I couldn't stop staring. The resemblance to Erica. It was uncanny, like she'd been reincarnated from the woman herself, the woman who was still alive.

She giggled, the serious look on her face turning bubbly within seconds. "Silly duckling," she whispered, her voice sweet and angelic.

Duckling? I thought. *That's what Erica used to call me.*

"Who are you?" I demanded again, my tone still clearly not strong enough to scare her away.

"Silly, I'm Noelle. I just told you!" She giggled again.

"I don't see what's so funny."

Her cheeks blushed red, as if I'd embarrassed her somehow, the smile on her face gone.

"I'm sorry. You're just so cute when you're confused. I didn't mean to laugh at you." She leaned in and gave me a kiss on the cheek. My body tingled at the feeling of her touch, as if it were reacting to it. "I'm Noelle," she whispered again. "And I've been looking everywhere for you."

BUZZ!

The sound of my alarm clock startled me, and I nearly fell out of bed. When I finally regained my composure, I found myself back in my disgustingly plain room. The tree, the ornaments, the fake snow, the red walls, they were all gone. I turned my head from side to side. And Noelle, she was nowhere to be found.

It must've just been a dream. I really should lay off that whiskey.

My head was pounding when I rolled out of bed. I fumbled with my alarm clock until I figured out how to shut it off. And when I finally got a chance to take a good look at it, I saw the date. Great. Eleven days before Christmas.

I'd been dreading Christmas this year. My mother said she'd found someone, the daughter of a neighbor she thought would make a perfect wife for me. And if I didn't at least meet her, she'd disown me. I knew she was kidding, but the woman wasn't getting any younger, and I figured I owed her at least that much.

But I couldn't get Noelle out of my head. That dream had felt so real, the touch of her delicate fingers so natural that it felt like I was living two lives: the one I dreaded in reality, and the one I craved in my dream. It still didn't make any sense to me. To this day, I don't think it'll ever make sense to me, why she looked so similar to Erica. All I knew was, I had to see her again.

That night, I sat out on my balcony and smoked a cigarette, followed by a bottle of whiskey. I needed to repeat exactly what I did the night before if I had any chance of seeing Noelle again. I needed to find out more, who she was, and why she had suddenly decided to make an appearance in my life.

When my nerves finally settled, and I fell asleep, I found myself sitting in that same room, obnoxiously decorated with sparkling tinsel and stockings hanging on the walls. There was a glass of eggnog sitting on the coffee table, and I lifted it up to take a sip. Delicious! The best eggnog I'd ever had in my entire life.

"Do you like it?" Noelle startled me when she walked in, holding a small box wrapped in snowflake wrapping paper with a large red bow on top.

"Uh huh," I managed to get out, the liquid still in my mouth as I struggled not to choke.

She smiled. "I'm glad."

Then she sat down beside me on the red velvet couch, and I could smell the sweet aroma of perfume she had on her body. She smelled like an angel sent down from Heaven, and I felt like I had died.

"This is for you," she said, handing me the present.

"For me?" I asked, confused. "But it's not Christmas yet."

She giggled. "I know. Just open it."

I grabbed the box from her delicate hands, our fingers touching in the process and sending a shiver of tingles up and down my body. She continued to look at me as I opened it, my face blushing at the embarrassment. Inside the neatly wrapped box, which I had torn open like a hungry beast, was a wrist watch.

"Wow!" I exclaimed. "Is this really for me?"

She nodded, her smile growing larger. "Read the back."

I turned the watch around, and engraved on the back were the words: Max and Noelle Forever.

"I... I don't understand," I said to her, turning my body in her direction.

"You will... soon enough."

The sound of my alarm blared again, and this time, I did fall out of bed. December 16th. Another day, another shitty day. I looked down at my wrist, expecting the dream to stay a dream, but right there, decorating my left wrist, was the same watch Noelle had just given me.

I didn't know what was happening, with my dream, with Noelle. But the more I saw her, the more I felt pulled to her. And none of it made any sense, the strange tie between fantasy and reality. Who was she? And how'd a gift I'd received in my dream appear in reality? I questioned it at first, tempted to call the cops and tell them someone's been sneaking into my apartment through a dream, but I was pretty sure they'd just laugh at me. A magical watch given to me by someone in my dream? It was crazy for *me* to even think it. But soon, as the days continued to go by, I stopped questioning it. I stopped trying to fight it. Noelle truly *was* the best thing that had ever happened to me, and I couldn't risk anything that would ruin that.

Every night for the next seven nights, I continued to repeat my patterns of behavior, anxiously rushing through the day just so I could down that bottle of whiskey and fall asleep to see her. I started to grow closer and closer to Noelle, not just physically, but it felt as if our brains just connected. It was as if she *was* Erica, but a hundred times better. It felt strange to think at the time, but I had fallen in love with her.

And on that seventh day, two days before Christmas, we finally kissed. To be honest, I'd wanted to kiss her on day two, but I didn't want to scare her away. She was just so perfect, and after what had happened with Erica, I didn't think I'd ever fall in love again. For the past three years, I'd had it in my plans to simply die alone, with or without a dog. I hadn't decided yet, but definitely not with a woman.

"You have no idea how much I've wanted to do that," I said to her when I gently pushed away.

We were both standing by the beautifully decorated tree, the twinkling lights brightening my day and bringing back the joy I used to have when it came to Christmas. The music playing on the radio lifted the terrible mood I'd been in during work that day, and the sparkling tinsel against the reflection of the chandelier no longer made me want to puke.

"I do know," she replied. "Because I've wanted to do the same ever since I first saw you. We belong together, Max. You and I. This is destiny."

"It is. It really, really is." I leaned in to kiss her again, my hands wrapping around her waist and pulling her body close to mine.

I'd never noticed it before, but her body was no less than a perfect twenty, and when she pressed against me, it felt like we completed a puzzle.

It felt as if my life was finally complete.

Chapter Three

Buzz! I woke up to the sound of my alarm, falling out of bed once again. But instead of the frustration that usually came after, I was happy. I was actually happy to be alive. I now had something worth living for. And that something was Noelle. I eagerly jumped out of bed and skipped into the shower, brushing my teeth while humming to

Jingle Bells. Tomorrow was finally Christmas, and I couldn't wait to spend it with Noelle.

"You look chipper today," my co-worker, Steve, said to me when I walked into the office.

I had a steaming hot cup of cocoa in my hand and Noelle's Santa hat perched on top of my head, still humming the same song.

"I am," I said with a grin as I threw my briefcase on top of my desk.

"Care to share?"

"I met someone. A girl."

I originally had no intention of telling anyone about Noelle, afraid that they'd think I had gone crazy, but I felt so ecstatic that I could no longer keep it to myself. I winced as soon as those words left my mouth, and prepared myself for jabs and ridicules, the works. For the past three years, I'd gone on and on about never dating again, swearing off women and relationships forever, that I would never again let some broad dictate my life and change it. And now, here I was, grinning like a monkey getting its butt scratched and skipping down the halls of the office.

"Congrats, man," Steve said instead, patting me on the back. "It's 'bout time you get back on the market. We were all rooting for you." He perched himself on top of my desk. "So, who's the lucky gal? Anyone I know?"

I glared at him. "Anyone you know? Does it look like we know the same people?"

He shrugged. "No, but it never hurts to ask. The world's a lot smaller than you think."

I shook my head. So wrong. His words were so wrong, in so many ways.

"Her name's Noelle. We've been seeing each other for about two weeks now, and we had our first kiss last night. It's going pretty well. And no, it's *not* someone you know."

"She hot? Any hot friends? Come on, man. I need details!"

"Why?"

"Because...," he said smoothly, "if you ever get dumped by this one too, I'd like to know what my chances are."

"Get the fuck out of here." I rolled my eyes and pushed him over.

But for the rest of the day, I couldn't stop thinking about what he'd said. I mean, Noelle *was* hot. But that also meant there was a high chance of her leaving me, just like Erica did. I'll admit, I'm not the most handsome man in the world, but I treat women right, and that's what I'd been priding myself on. But then again, Erica left, so it clearly hadn't been working.

I grew more and more anxious over the course of that day. The thought of losing the girl of my dream to another man was too unbearable to even think about. I wasn't even sure if I ever got over Erica, the person I thought was my forever; I'd simply replaced her with Noelle. If I were to lose her too, I wasn't sure what I'd do with myself.

Then I chuckled at my thoughts. Why was I so worried about losing her? She lived in my dream, a figment of my imagination. However strange that dream had been, mixing with reality, there's no way she could leave me. It was impossible!

That night, I lied in bed with her present in my hands and fell asleep. I'd gotten her a diamond bracelet, carved with our initials on it. If she was able to give me a watch through my dream, I didn't see why I wouldn't be able to give her a bracelet through reality. And to top it off, I had attached a single rose on top, a single rose to signify our love for each other.

It didn't take long before I found myself back in that room, that red-walled room covered in tinsel and stockings. But I was happy to see them. Christmas was only a few hours away, and I was excited for the chance to spend it with Noelle.

But she didn't show up. After two hours of sitting on that red velvet couch, my best iron-pressed suit beginning to crease, she still didn't show. I didn't understand. I did everything the same, a cigarette, whiskey, even forced myself to smash the glass bottle and hold it against my wrist, so why wasn't she here?

Maybe she's just running late, I foolishly thought to myself. *She'll show. I know she will.*

Four hours had passed, and I still stupidly held that gift box on my lap. I couldn't even smell the freshly-baked cookies or eggnog that she usually had ready for me. But still, I continued to sit there, waiting and waiting for her, a smile still resting on my face. It wasn't like I could leave, even if I wanted to. But I didn't. I kept telling myself that she'd show. Just waiting. Waiting. Waiting.

BUZZ!

My alarm rang the next morning, Christmas Day, and I woke up in my own bed, with the boring white sheets. The single red rose and ugly wrapped gift box had both fallen onto the floor when I rolled over in the middle of the night.

Just my luck. I finally found a woman I wanted to spend my life with, and of course, she'd left, just like all the others. I was devastated! Hate began to boil in my blood, and I threw the gift into the trash before throwing my sheets off my body. I stormed into the living room, which I had neatly decorated with whatever last-minute trinkets and a fake plastic tree I managed to get from the dollar store, and threw them all into a trash bag. I didn't want anything to do with Christmas, or Noelle, or anyone, for that matter.

The office was closed for Christmas, giving me an excuse to not leave my apartment. But even if it wasn't, I would've called in sick. I felt as if my heart was breaking. Every day, ever since I first met Noelle, I started to believe that there was hope in my life again, that things were finally going to turn around for me. I'd even joined in on holiday conversations in the office and bought several gifts for my nephew. Now, they sat in the same trash bag as the rest of the useless junk.

My phone dinged, and a message from Mark popped up, asking me when I'd arrive at our parents for Christmas lunch. I immediately deleted his message and threw my phone across the room. Fat chance in hell was I gonna go over now. Everything was ruined, and it was all Noelle's fault. I hated her! Why'd she have to come into my life if she was just going to walk right back out?

My phone dinged again, then once more, but I ignored it and went into the kitchen to grab a pack of cigarettes and a bottle of whiskey. After Erica left me, I'd stocked up on more whiskey than I'd ever need in a lifetime. But it didn't bother me. Can never have too many. And as I walked back out, I picked up a knife.

Sitting out on my balcony, under the blinding sun, and listening to the sickening sound of laughing children out on the street, I took several swigs from the bottle and leaned back with a cigarette in my mouth. Time to feel sorry for myself again. I didn't know what I had done wrong in my life to deserve all this. My heart was barely even healed before it had gotten broken again. I was only twenty-five, but I'd felt like I'd experienced enough pain for a lifetime.

The knife. I didn't bring it out for no reason. While everyone else was too busy celebrating a holiday that had turned into pure greed, I was suffering alone. And I liked it that way. Less messy, and less to explain.

"I loved you, Noelle. Why didn't you just fucking show up?"

Tears continued to pour down my cheeks as the knife came closer to my wrist. I was really going to do it this time. I was really done with all these games. No more. I'd had enough.

Suddenly, my doorbell rang, pulling me away from my plan. Grumbling, I knew it had to be Mark, or my mom, or someone else who had come to throw their happiness in my face. I didn't want to answer. I just wanted to end it right there, the pain too over-whelming to bear. But what if it was important? What if someone in my family had an accident, and I'd chosen to off myself instead?

The bell rang again while I paced back and forth

with my thoughts. Eventually giving in, I put the knife down to go answer it.

"Don't go anywhere," I said to the knife. "I'll be back."

I was still in my pajamas, baggy stained sweats and an old T-shirt, but whatever, it wasn't like I had anyone to impress. The bell rang once more.

"Hold on!" I yelled. "Chill the fuck out!"

Kicking aside the phone that had been thrown, I swung open the door, and my jaw dropped.

"Merry Christmas, Max Miller!"

I couldn't believe it. Sitting outside, on top of the hood of my car, and dressed in the most adorable Christmas outfit, was Noelle. Could it really be? I blinked and pinched myself several times, but the sting assured me that this wasn't a dream. She was really here. Noelle was really here! Live, in person, sitting outside my apartment.

All this time, I thought she was only part of my dream. Never did I ever wonder whether she really existed. I mean, it made sense. The touch of her body felt so real... so did her breath against my ear, and... and the watch! I didn't care how. I didn't care why. I didn't care that just minutes before, I hated her.

Tears of joy welled in my eyes, and I ran over to embrace her in my arms. She felt so real, like she had felt when I first held her. I felt the warmth beginning to come back inside my chest, my heart beating faster and faster as she pressed against me and snuggled her nose in my neck. I didn't want to let go. I didn't ever want to let go. Ever. My neighbors all stared at me like I was a lunatic, but I didn't care. All I cared about was the woman in my arms.

"Max, I—" She started to speak, but I pressed my lips against hers and interrupted whatever she was going to say.

None of that matter at this moment. I wanted to kiss her, taste her, make up for all the lost hours we could've spent together. My frustration toward her absence had disappeared. Her lips felt so warm and soothing against mine that I wanted to kiss her forever.

When I finally pulled away, five long minutes later, my arms were still wrapped around her. I still feared that as soon as I let go, she'd disappear again, and I couldn't have that. Not again. My heart couldn't handle another one.

"Max, I—" She started to speak again.

"I love you!" I blurted out, interrupting her once again.

But she didn't get mad. Instead, she threw her arms around my neck and smacked her lips hard against mine.

"I love you too, Max! And I want to apologize for not showing up last night. I was trying to make it a surprise by showing up on your front door instead, for Christmas, to show you that dreams can come true. I hope you're not angry with me."

I had been angry, but I wasn't going to tell her that. It wasn't like telling her would make me feel any better. It'd just make both of us feel that much worse.

I shook my head and smiled at her. "I'm not angry with you at all. I love you so much."

The sun was starting to melt the snowfall from the night before. It was rare for Arizona to gather so much snow, something that only happened once every few years, but despite the chilly air that brushed against my cold skin, I loved that it was a White Christmas, a perfect Christmas.

My body shivered, suddenly realizing how cold it

actually was. "Let's go inside," I told her, leading her inside with one arm still around her waist.

I didn't let go of her when we walked through the front door and into the living room. I didn't let go of her until I led her into my bedroom and laid her down on top of my sheets, and then climbed over her to kiss her even more. I wasn't sure what had possessed me. I wasn't usually like this, so forward, usually shyer and more reserved when it came to women. But with Noelle, I felt like she'd been mine for years, the lust that I had toward her so overpowering that I didn't want to stop until I felt myself inside her.

"I love you, Noelle, I love you so fucking much." I pulled off her Santa hat and ruffled my fingers through her chestnut brown hair, and then slid my fingers down to the zipper of her boots and undid them. When my fingers finally made their way back up, they went slowly, grazing up and down her bare legs before reaching up her upper thigh and under her short dress.

She didn't hesitate. Unlike Erica when we made love for the first time, Noelle didn't hesitate, as if we'd done this many times before.

The next twenty minutes was the most pleasurable moment of my entire life thus far. Our bodies intertwined between my sheets, and she whispered her moans in my ear as I gently gestured my hip between her legs. She was fragile, a snow globe I never wanted to break, and when I finished, so did she, our two bodies becoming one.

"That was amazing," I sighed when we separated and had our backs against the bed. Her head was resting on my bare chest, and I continued to run my fingers through her hair.

"Best feeling ever," she chimed. "Do you know that you're my first?"

"No kidding! Really?" Hearing her say that made this moment that much more special.

"Yes." She nodded. "And I want you to be my only."

Before I could respond, my doorbell rang again. This time, I was sure it someone coming to fetch me for Christmas lunch.

"I'll be right back," I said, kissing her on the forehead and throwing my clothes on.

When I swung open the door, Mark was standing there with his wife, Shanna.

"What the hell, man? Why you screening my calls? I've been trying to reach you all morning."

"Sorry." I rubbed the back of my neck. It felt like someone was running their fingers up and down it, but no one was behind me. "I couldn't find my phone."

"You mean that phone?" Mark pointed to the spot beside my feet, where the screen of my phone had slightly cracked from when I threw it.

"Uh... yeah... I guess."

"And why do you have so many garbage bags laying around? You know trash day isn't until Wednesday, right?"

"Huh?" I looked around my living room, almost forgetting that I had bagged up all my Christmas decorations. "Yeah... I guess I forgot."

"I swear, sometimes I wonder how you're the smart one in the family." Mark shook his head. "Anyway, Mom and Dad are waiting for you. Everyone's already there. Come on! You can ride with us."

"Actually, I think I'm going to drive myself." I then turned my head around and spotted Noelle's black boots. "And I think I'm gonna bring someone. A girl."

Shanna beamed with happiness, like she was even more excited than I was about this. "Oh my god! You finally did it? You finally got a girlfriend?"

"Yeah, I guess I did."

She threw her arms around me and gave me a quick hug. "I'm so happy for you! Mark keeps saying you'll die alone, but I had faith in you."

"Geez, thanks, babe. Way to sell me out," Mark joked at his wife. Then he turned his attention back to me. "But yeah, man, bring her. I'm sure Mom will love to meet the special chick that captured her favorite son's heart. But make it quick. Everyone's starving!"

"I'll be there in thirty." I saluted him and closed the door.

Noelle was still naked beneath the sheets when I returned. God, she looked more beautiful every time I saw her.

"Who was that?" she asked.

"My brother, Mark." I climbed back into bed and kissed her on the cheek. "How would you like to come with me to my parents for Christmas lunch? The whole family will be there, and I'm sure they'd be thrilled to meet you."

She blushed. "I don't know. What if they don't like me? I don't want them to hate you too for being with me."

"Nah." I kissed her again. "I love you, and I promise you they will, too."

Exactly thirty minutes later, Noelle and I were standing outside my parents' house. I'd fished the presents out from the trash bag and loaded them into the trunk of my car. I looked over at Noelle, who looked perfectly comfortable in her short sleeveless dress, while I was freezing my ass off. I didn't know how she did it. Like the cold didn't even bother her.

It took two rings before Mom swung open the door and greeted me.

"Max! I'm so glad you could make it!" She gave me a hug and a quick peck on the cheek.

I hugged her back. "Thanks for having me, Mom." I gestured over to Noelle, my fingers wrapped around hers. "This is Noelle, my girlfriend."

But instead of another happy grin on her face and a hug for Noelle, her smile turned into a frown, and she looked at me as if I had just grown a tail.

"Come on in! Everyone's waiting!" she said instead, turning her back and walking inside.

That's weird,

I thought. *Why was she so cold to Noelle?*

"I told you no one would like me," Noelle whispered beside me as I led her inside.

But I brushed it off. "Nah, I'm sure it was just a misunderstanding. She's probably stressed out from all the cooking. I'm sure the rest of the family will find you delightful."

We walked into the dining room to find everyone already seated, with two empty chairs remaining for Noelle and I. As we sat down, the rest of the crowd was already digging into their food, so I scooped up a spoonful of mashed potatoes for Noelle, and then one for myself.

"Delicious, Ma, really," I said to my mother, who gave me a nod and tended to my nephew who had spilled gravy all over his nice shirt.

"So, Max," Mark said when he noticed my presence. "Where's this girlfriend of yours? She running late?"

I lowered my brows at him. Was he kidding me? What the hell's wrong with my family? "Um... she's right next to me?" I pointed over to Noelle, who gave Mark a shy wave.

"Huh? What are you talking about? That's Grandma. Unless you two have something going on that no one else knows about."

I watched as Grandma opened her eyes in horror and quickly shook her head before returning to her potatoes. "No, not Grandma. Noelle, she's literally sitting right next to me. Why are you being so rude?"

That's when Dad sat in the seat beside me... right on top of Noelle.

"Hey, son, I've been meani—"

"Dad! Get off! You're sitting on her!" I jumped up and yelled, pulling my father off my girlfriend.

"Whoa! Whoa! Sorry! I thought that seat was empty."

"What the hell is wrong with all of you?!" I shouted at my family. "After three years, three fucking years, I finally find love again, and you're all acting like assholes! If you don't want to welcome Noelle into the family, then I won't be part of it, either." I grabbed her by the hand. "Come on, Noelle. Let's get out of here."

"Max, wait!" Mom called after me.

"Save it, Mom. I'm done." I slammed the front door behind me and opened the passenger door for Noelle before climbing into the driver's seat and pulling out of the driveway. Not once did I try to look back.

Epilogue

Looking back, I should've seen it as a red flag when Mark said no one was there. My whole family was just looking out for me, concerned about my mental health. But I was too stubborn to believe them, too stubborn to listen to anyone else but myself.

"Let's move," Noelle had said to me during the drive home.

"Move? To where?"

"The North Pole. Alaska. I feel like that's where I belong, with the cold. I don't like the warm weather here. It makes me feel sad."

Just the thought of having to live somewhere with temperature that dropped down into the negatives sent chills throughout my body. But Noelle meant everything to me, and if she wanted to move to Alaska, then I'd have to suck it up and move there with her.

So, a week later, we loaded our things into my car and headed north, driving for nearly six days before we finally arrived at a beat-up log cabin up in the mountains.

"I used to live here," Noelle said, "when I was just a little girl. It's been so long I almost forgot what it looks like."

I walked around the dilapidated building and took in the sights. There was definitely a musky smell to the place, like it had been left abandoned for decades. It also looked like one swift blow of a blizzard would send the whole place down to the ground. But Noelle seemed so happy, playing in the snow like an innocent child, and I was willing to do anything for her, including fixing up the place as much as I could to make it livable.

That was three weeks ago. Three long weeks before I finally got past my lovesick ways and realized that Noelle wasn't real. That she was never real to begin with. She wasn't real when she appeared at my front door Christmas morning, and she wasn't real when I brought her over to my parents. No wonder no one could see her. She didn't exist. But I'd wanted so much for her to exist that I made myself believe that the person I saw in my dream was a real person.

The first few days after moving into this cabin was just as expected. Happily in love and sharing every moment together. I had enough savings to care for both of us for at least a couple months before I had to venture out and get a job. Sands wasn't thrilled when I mailed my resignation to him while staying at a hotel in Montana. But it had to be done. I had to follow my heart, and that was with Noelle.

But soon, tension started to grow between us. She grew more and more distant as so did I, the cold numbing my brain as much as it was numbing the skin on my body. And two weeks later, I woke up, and she was gone. Not a single word or note was left about where she was going, and there were no signs of where she had gone, as if she had just vanished. That's when I started to see the signs.

Why is it that the one person I finally fall in love with after Erica turns out to be just an illusion? I had wanted Erica back in my life for so long that I somehow created an alternative version of her instead, in the form of Noelle, forcing myself to believe that she could be more than just a dream.

But even now, even as I find myself freezing in this cabin alone, with a rusty immobile vehicle outside and no one to hold for warmth, I still want her back. And I'll do anything to see her again, to hold her again. I'd given up my entire life for this woman, and I'm not about to walk away with nothing.

I finished the last sips of my tea. The supplies I'd brought with me are beginning to either spoil or dwindle, but I didn't care. I'm too burnt out. Placing my mug down, I retreat to my bed, throwing a warm robe over my body and climbing in under the sheets.

Slowly, I close my eyes and let my body fall to sleep.

"Welcome home, Max." And there she is, Noelle, dressed in that same Santa hat and cute little dress she'd always worn, standing in a place that resembles a more picture-perfect version of the cabin I was in.

Lights decorated the crimson red walls. Eggnog and a platter of chocolate chip cookies sat on the glass coffee table. And a large evergreen tree stood by the fireplace, twinkling with tinsel and sparkling lights. I pick up a cookie and walk over to the red velvet couch, sitting down beside my beautiful girlfriend.

"Merry Christmas." I smile, leaning over to kiss her.

The End

45

About the Author

Viola Tempest is a dystopian fantasy and paranormal romance author who yearns to expose the truth of those in the modern world: the good, the bad, and the ugly. Her inspiration primarily stems from life experiences, those who annoy her, ex-boyfriends, and the crazy dreams that pop into her head every once in a while.

Stalk her below!

* * *

Website:
https://www.violatempest.com/

Facebook Page:
https://www.facebook.com/authorviolatempest

Instagram:
https://www.instagram.com/author_violatempest/

Goodreads:
https://www.goodreads.com/author/show/21693342.
Viola_Tempest

Bookbub:
https://www.bookbub.com/authors/viola-tempest

Dreaming of NOELLE

ENCHANTED WISHES COLLECTION

VIOLA TEMPEST